Arabian Nights

The Ruined Man Who Became Rich

Indrani Vohra

Om KIDZ
An imprint of Om Books International

Once upon a time, there lived in Baghdad a wealthy man who had lost all his money and become so poor that he could barely afford a meal a day. One night, while he slept, he saw in his dream a man, who said to him, 'Your fortune lies in Cairo. Go there and seek it.'

The man went to Cairo. By the time he arrived, it was already evening. So, he decided to seek refuge at a mosque for the night.

The same night, a group of bandits entered the mosque and made their way into the adjoining house. The owners of the house heard them come in and cried out for help. The police came to their aid. The bandits

ran away, but the police kept searching all over. They entered the mosque, and on finding the man from Baghdad, got hold of him and beat him up. They thought it was he who had tried to rob the house next door.

They put the poor man into jail. After three days, the police chief sent for him and asked him, 'Where are you from?' The man answered, 'I am from Baghdad.' The chief looked at him with a quizzical expression on his face. 'What brought you to Cairo?'

He asked. The man replied, ‘I saw a dream where a man said to me that my fortune lies in Cairo. So I came here to get it. But the fortune he had promised me turned out to be the generous beating you gave me!’

The chief laughed and said, 'O dear man, I have seen a dream thrice where a man said to me, "There is in Baghdad a house with a large courtyard and a garden that surrounds it. At the lower end of it is a beautiful fountain under which is buried a fortune. Go and get it." But I am wise enough to know it is just a dream.'

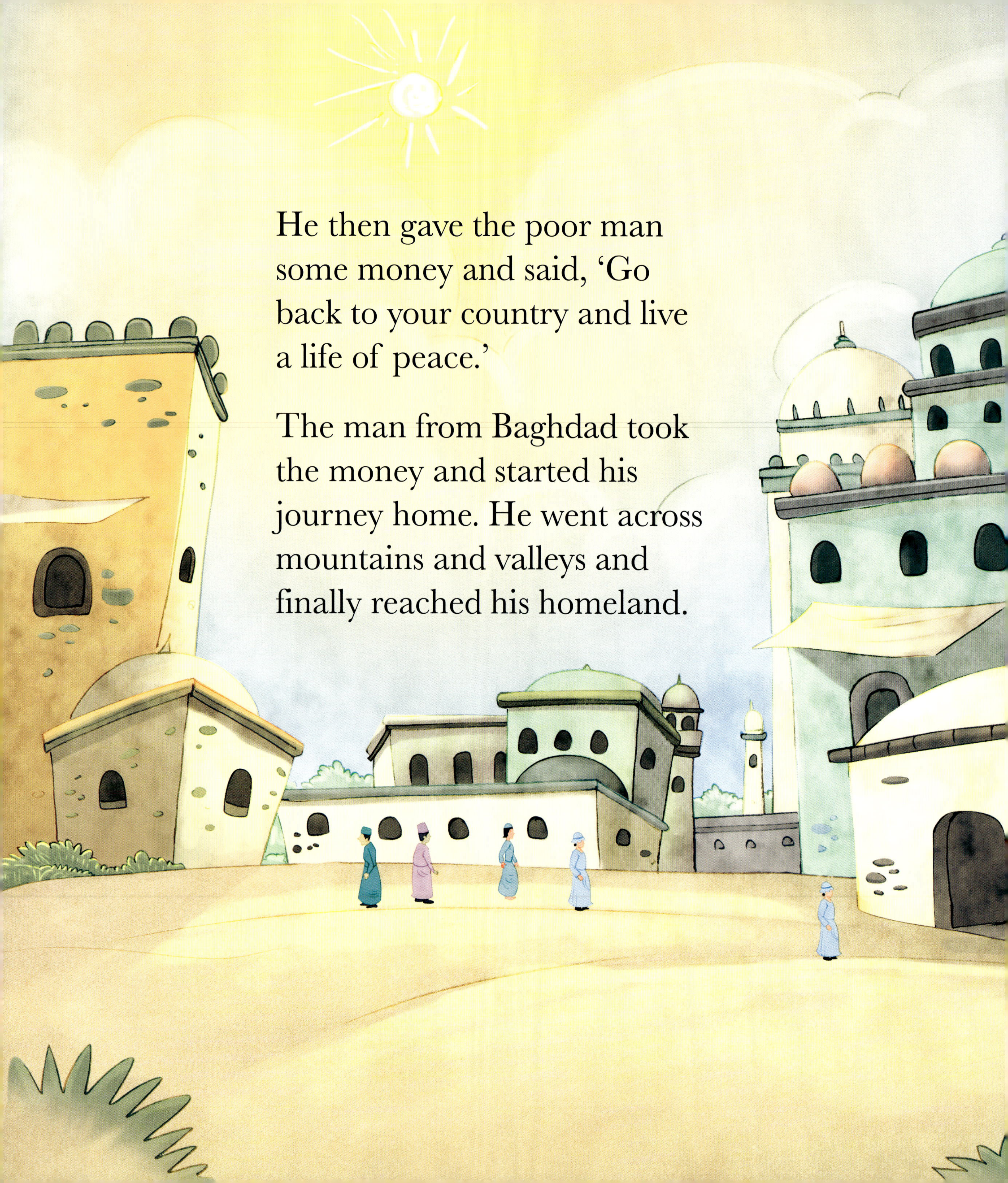

He then gave the poor man some money and said, 'Go back to your country and live a life of peace.'

The man from Baghdad took the money and started his journey home. He went across mountains and valleys and finally reached his homeland.

Now, the house in Baghdad that the chief had described belonged to the poor man when he was rich. The poor man thought, ‘Why don’t I dig underneath the fountain in my garden? Maybe there is a fortune in store for me.’ He did so and to his utter surprise, there lay a treasure of gold under the fountain!

He couldn't believe his eyes! Finally, God had heard his prayers and bestowed him with wealth. With his newfound treasure, the man made a bigger house with a bigger garden. He bought a new horse for himself and endless gifts for the poor living in the city of Baghdad. The man was simply elated and now lived a life of comfort and joy.

He looked up towards the sky and thanked God for blessing him with this abundant fortune and a great destiny. He was, indeed, the ruined man who became rich again!